15 JUN 2022

13 JAN 2024

GW01549764

Renew this item at:
http://library.sheffield.gov.uk
or contact your local library

LIBRARIES, ARCHIVES & INFORMATION

215109237

Craig Starts Cookery
Copyright © Colleen Speight and Neil Wilkinson 2013

First published and distributed in 2013 by Gatehouse Media Limited

ISBN: 978-1-84231-086-1

British Library Cataloguing-in-Publication Data:
A catalogue record for this book is available from the British Library

No part of this publication may be reproduced in any form or by any means, electronic, mechanical, photocopying, recording or otherwise, without the prior written consent of the publishers.

Craig is sitting in his cell thinking about food.

"I'm hungry."

"Would you like to take the cookery course, Craig?"

"I don't know. I have never tried cookery."

"There is a space on our course –

shall I put your name down?"

"Do you cook burgers?" asks Craig.

"Yes, sometimes, and lots of other dishes.

Would you like to try it?"

"Alright then," says Craig.

Craig sits at the table and listens to the tutor.

"What are we making today?" he asks.

"We're cooking all-day breakfast today," replies the tutor.

"Come and collect your food, everyone."

Craig collects his food from the tutor and takes it to his work area.

He is busy cooking the bacon.

"This bacon smells really good –

it's going to be tasty!"

At last it is ready – all-day breakfast!

"This is tasty, what is next?" asks Craig.

"Washing-up!" says the tutor.

Activity 1: Copy the sentences

Copy the sentences onto the lines below including the punctuation (. , ! " ? ' -)

1. Craig is sitting in his cell thinking about food. "I'm hungry."

2. "Would you like to take the cookery course, Craig?"

3. "I don't know. I have never tried cookery."

4. "There is a space on our course – shall I put your name down?"

5. "Do you cook burgers?" asks Craig.

Activity 2: Copy the sentences

Copy the sentences onto the lines below including the punctuation (. , ! " ? ' -)

1. "Yes, sometimes, and lots of other dishes. Would you like to try it?"

2. "Alright then," says Craig.

3. Craig sits at the table and listens to the tutor. "What are we making today?" he asks.

4. "We're cooking all-day breakfast today," replies the tutor.
"Come and collect your food, everyone."

Activity 3: Copy the sentences

Copy the sentences onto the lines below including the punctuation (. , ! " ? ' -)

1. Craig collects his food from the tutor and takes it to his work area.

2. He is busy cooking the bacon. "This bacon smells really good – it's going to be tasty!"

3. At last it is ready – all-day breakfast!

4. "This is tasty, what is next?" asks Craig. "Washing-up!" says the tutor.

Activity 4: Missing words

Choose the missing words from the box below to complete the sentences.

1. Craig is sitting in his cell _____ about food. "I'm _____ ."

2. "Would you like to take the _____ course, Craig?"

3. "I _____ know. I have _____ tried cookery."

4. "There is a _____ on our course – shall I put your _____ down?"

5. "Do you cook _____?" asks Craig.

6. "Yes, sometimes, and lots of other _____ ."

7. "Would you like to _____ it?"

8. "Alright then," says _____ .

| try   hungry   don't   cookery   never   Craig |
| space   thinking   name   burgers   dishes |

Activity 5: Missing words

Choose the missing words from the box below
to complete the sentences.

1. "What are we _____ today?" he asks.

2. "We're cooking _____ breakfast today,"
   replies the tutor.

3. "Come and _____ your food, everyone."

4. Craig collects his _____ from the tutor
   and takes it to his _____ area.

5. He is _____ cooking the _____ . "This bacon
   _____ really good – it's going to be tasty."

6. At last it is ready – all-day _____ !

7. "This is _____ , what is next?" asks _____ .

8. "Washing-up!" says the _____ .

tutor	tasty	Craig	breakfast	food	busy	
collect	work	all-day	making	smells	bacon	

17

Activity 6: All about Craig

Circle the correct word.

1. **Craig feels** tired / hungry / happy.

2. **Craig is taking a course in**
   joinery / cookery / painting.

3. **There is a** mistake / space / plate **on the course.**

4. **What are we** choosing / making / peeling?

5. **We're cooking all-day** breakfast / tea / dinner.

6. **Craig collects his food from the**
   cooker / fridge / tutor.

7. **He takes the food to his** room / play / work **area.**

8. **The bacon is going to be** nasty / tasty / pasty.

9. **At last it is** gone / eaten / ready **– all-day breakfast!**

10. **Next, the** dishing / washing / mopping **– up!**

Activity 7: Craig is mixed up!

Put the words in the correct order to make a sentence. Add capital letters and punctuation.

1. craig sitting in is cell about food thinking his

   _____

2. course cookery craig to take the you like would

   _____

   _____

3. burgers you cook do

   _____

4. i put name shall your down

   _____

5. it try you like would to

   _____

6. are today making what we asks he

   _____

Activity 8: Craig is still in a muddle!

Put the words in the correct order to make a sentence. Add capital letters and punctuation.

1. all-day cooking we're today breakfast

   _____

2. from food collects his the tutor craig

   _____

3. good really bacon smells this

   _____

4. tasty be going it's to

   _____

5. is ready - at last it all-day breakfast

   _____

6. craig tasty is this next is what asks

   _____

7. the tutor washing-up says

   _____

Activity 9: Craig's all-day breakfast

Answer these questions. Write full sentences with capital letters and punctuation.

1. **Name four items of food Craig had in his breakfast.**

   _____

2. **How did the bacon smell when it was cooking?**

   _____

3. **What do you think Craig wanted to make?**

   _____

4. **Do you think Craig enjoyed cooking? Why?**

   _____

5. **Do you enjoy cooking? What do you like to cook?**

   _____

   _____

6. **Describe <u>your</u> favourite meal. Write at least two sentences.**

   _____

   _____

If you have enjoyed this book, why not try one of these other titles from Gatehouse Books:

Tom's Travels　　　　　　　　　　ISBN: 978-1-84231-079-3
by Colleen Speight & Neil Wilkinson

Tom is in prison. He wants to learn to read. The first book in the *Inside Reading* series.

Dean Becomes a Dad　　　　　　　ISBN: 978-1-84231-085-4
by Colleen Speight & Neil Wilkinson

Dean is in prison. He gets some good news from his girlfriend. The second book in the *Inside Reading* series.

Bob's Problem　　　　　　　　　　ISBN: 978-1-84231-056-4
by Margaret Adams

Bob likes his job on the dairy counter at Asco supermarket, but his boss has other plans for him. Bob is forced to reveal his problem. Then one day, a shocking event puts Bob's life on the line.

Dan's Dinner　　　　　　　　　　　ISBN: 978-1-84231-064-9
by Margaret Adams

Dan, a supermarket employee, is a refugee who has had terrible and sad things happen in his past. One day something happens that may well change his future.

Gatehouse Books®

Gatehouse Books are written for older teenagers and adults who are developing their basic reading and writing or English language skills.

The format of our books is clear and uncluttered.
The language is familiar and the text is often line-broken, so that each line ends at a natural pause.

Gatehouse Books are widely used within Adult Basic Education throughout the English speaking world. They are also a valuable resource within the Prison Education Service and Probation Services, Social Services and secondary schools - both in basic skills and ESOL teaching situations.

Catalogue available

Gatehouse Media Limited
PO Box 965
Warrington
WA4 9DE

Tel/Fax: 01925 267778
E-mail: info@gatehousebooks.com
Website: www.gatehousebooks.com